On her birthday, Little Mo's parents invited her friends over for a big celebration.

小默的生日到了，爸爸妈妈邀请了小默的朋友们一起来庆祝。

The Magical Silkworm

This book is edited and designed by the Editorial Committee of *Cultural China* series.

Story and Illustrations: Lin Xin
Translation: Yijin Wert

Copy Editor: Shelly Bryant
Editor: Cao Yue
Editorial Director: Zhang Yicong

Senior Consultants: Sun Yong, Wu Ying, Yang Xinci
Managing Director and Publisher: Wang Youbu

ISBN: 978-1-60220-461-4

Address any comments about *The Magical Silkworm* to:

Better Link Press
99 Park Ave
New York, NY 10016
USA

or

Shanghai Press and Publishing Development Co., Ltd.
F 7 Donghu Road, Shanghai, China (200031)
Email: comments_betterlinkpress@hotmail.com

Printed in China by Shanghai Donnelley Printing Co., Ltd.

1 3 5 7 9 10 8 6 4 2

The Magical Silkworm

A Story about a Birthday Gift
Told in English and Chinese

By Lin Xin
Translated by Yijin Wert

Better Link Press

Little Mo's parents brought out their birthday gift for her—a mysterious box. Everyone there was very anxious to find out what was in the box.

爸爸妈妈拿出给小默的生日礼物——一个神秘的盒子。大家都期待地围了上去。

Excitedly, Little Mo opened the box, only to find some ugly caterpillars crawling on a bunch of green leaves.
"This gift is frightening!" Little Mo's friends muttered.

小默兴奋地打开盒子，却发现里边只有一群黑不溜秋的毛毛虫，在绿叶子上扭来扭去。

小伙伴们嘟囔着："这个礼物可怪吓人的。"

Little Mo was very disappointed.

小默失望极了。

"These are silkworm larvae. They love to eat mulberry leaves. They can spew out silk threads for making clothes ..." All her friends left before Little Mo's parents could finish their explanation.

"这是蚕宝宝，它们爱吃桑叶，会吐丝织衣……"没等爸爸妈妈说完，小朋友们都跑开了。

"This is the ugliest birthday present that I have ever seen!"
Little Mo could no longer wait for her parents' explanation.
Heartbroken, she ran out of the house.

"这是我见过的最难看的生日礼物了!" 不等爸爸妈妈解释, 小默就伤心地跑出了家门。

"Don't let the gift bother you. Let's go explore together," Little Mo's friends tried to cheer her up. Then they climbed into a dark tree hole ...

小伙伴们安慰她："别想你的礼物啦，我们一起去探险吧。"说着，他们便钻进了一个黑乎乎的的大树洞……

Emerging on the other side of the tree hole, they found a magical forest. Wow—there were so many kinds of plants, including many mulberry trees.

钻出树洞，他们发现了一片神奇的树林。哇——这里长着各种各样的植物，还有好多好多的桑树。

"Look! The leaves are covered with dark caterpillars. They look exactly like the gift that Little Mo received!"

"快看呀！树叶上到处都是黑乎乎的的毛毛虫，和小默的礼物一模一样呢！"

The boys climbed the big tree and shook the branches. The black silkworm larvae fell down like rain drops. Little Mo quickly caught them with big leaves.

男孩们爬上高高的大树，摇晃起树枝。黑色的蚕宝宝像下雨一样落下来。小默连忙用大叶子接住。

Suddenly, the silkworm larvae became completely white. They looked like they had lost their black coats.

忽然，蚕宝宝们脱掉了黑色的外衣，变得白白净净了。

Little Mo immediately brought over more mulberry leaves for the silkworm larvae. They grew bigger and bigger, and they became rounder and rounder. It was like a magic!

小默赶紧找来更多的桑叶给蚕宝宝吃。神奇的事情发生了，只见蚕宝宝越长越大，越变越胖。

Suddenly a little boy cried, "Oh, no! There is a hole in my new clothes. My mother will be mad! What can I do?" He burst into tears.

这时，有个小男孩叫起来："啊呀呀不好了! 我的新衣裳勾破了。妈妈肯定会生气的! 这可怎么办呢?" 他急得哭了起来。

An idea came to Little Mo.

小默突然想到了一个主意。

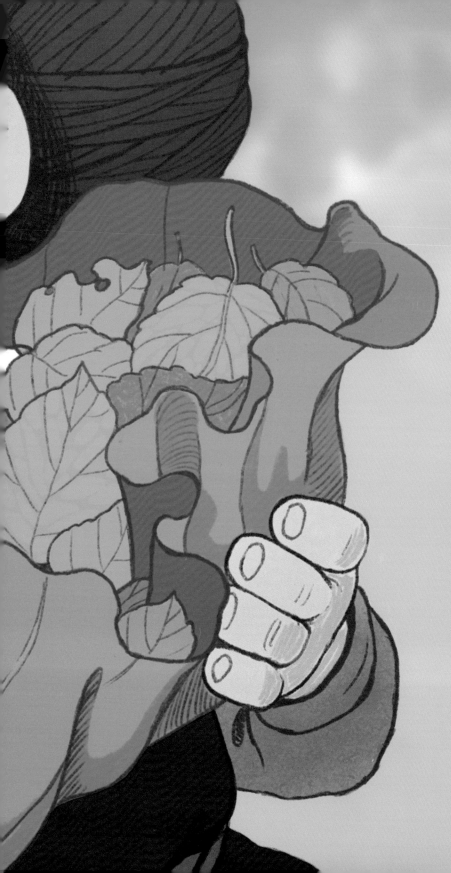

"Hello, silkworm baby, my parents told me that you can spew out thread for making clothes. Is that true?" Little Mo gently asked the silkworm larvae lying in her hands.

"Of course! The silk we produce is good for making clothes. Let us help you!" replied the round, white silkworm larvae.

"蚕宝宝，爸爸妈妈说你们会吐丝织衣，是真的吗？"小默轻轻地问手里的蚕宝宝。

白白胖胖的蚕宝宝说："当然！我们吐的丝可是做衣服的上好材料。让我们来帮助你们吧！"

The silkworm larvae immediately began to work. Some spewed out new threads while others constructed cocoons.

于是，蚕宝宝们忙碌起来，你吐丝来我作茧。

The boy put on his new silk clothes, which were light and cool. "Thank you! You are amazing, silkworm babies!"

男孩穿上崭新的丝绸衣裳，既轻薄又凉快。"蚕宝宝，谢谢你们，你们可真了不起！"

Squeezing back through the tree hole,
Little Mo rushed straight home.

从来时的树洞钻出去，小默一口气跑回家。

"Mom and Dad, I am so sorry. I didn't know that silkworms are actually so amazing!"

"Yes, Little Mo. You know that the silk quilts we use and the silk clothes we wear are all made of silk from silkworms."

"爸爸妈妈，对不起，我才知道原来蚕宝宝本领这么大！"

"是呀，小默。你看，我们盖的丝绸被子，穿的丝绸衣裳，可都是从蚕宝宝来的。"

Knowing that she had received the best birthday present ever, Little Mo grined from ear to ear.

小默感觉自己收获了一件最好的生日礼物，她甜甜地笑了。

Silk fabric is a textile made of silk threads produced by silkworms. It is a special product of China. China was the first country in the world to rear silkworm and reel silk. Chinese legend credited the invention of sericulture to the wife of the mythical Yellow Emperor named Leizu. During the Western Han dynasty (206 BC–AD 25), silk was exported in large quantities. Soon it became a world-renowned product of China. That's why the road to transport silk from China to foreign countries is called "the Silk Road."

丝绸是用蚕吐出的丝制作而成的纺织品，是中国的特产。中国是世界上最早驯育野蚕并缫丝织绸的国家，相传是黄帝的妻子嫘祖发明了养蚕。西汉时期，丝绸被不断地从中国大批运往海外，成为举世闻名的产品。那条将丝绸从中国运到国外的运输之路便被称为"丝绸之路"。